JUNIOR
GRAPHIC NOVEL

DISNEP PIRATES of the CARIBBEAN
DEAD MAN'S CHEST

Adapted by Stefano Ambrosio

Artwork by Giovanni Rigano
Igor Chimisso
Silvano Scolari
Andrea Cagol
Stefano Attardi
Carlotta Quattrocolo
Marco Ghiglione
Kawaii Creative Studio

Based on the screenplay written by Ted Elliott & Terry Rossio
Based on characters created by Ted Elliott & Terry Rossio
and Stuart Beattie and Jay Wolpert
Based on Walt Disney's Pirates of the Caribbean
Produced by Jerry Bruckheimer
Directed by Gore Verbinski

DISNEP PRESS

New York

Copyright © 2007 Disney Enterprises, inc.

No part of this book may be reproduced or transmitted in any form or by any means, electronic or mechanical, including photocopying, recording, or by any information storage and retrieval system, without written permission from the publisher. For information address Disney Press, 114 Fifth Avenue, New York, New York 10011-5690.

Printed in the United States of America
First U.S. Edition
3 5 7 9 10 8 6 4 2
Library of Congress Catalog Card Number 2006934264
ISBN-13: 978-1-4231-0370-7
ISBN-10: 1-4231-0370-X

3

4

PORT ROYAL.

NOT A GOOD DAY FOR A *WEDDING*.

MISTER TURNER, MISS SWANN, YOU ARE CHARGED WITH CONSPIRING TO RELEASE A CONVICT! PERHAPS YOU REMEMBER A CERTAIN *PIRATE* NAMED JACK SPARROW?

CAPTAIN JACK SPARROW!

A *CAPTAIN* SETS HIS SHIP'S COURSE.

BUT JACK'S *COMPASS* WON'T WORK, AND HE CAN'T FIND HIS WAY . . .

TIME'S RUN OUT, JACK.

BOOTSTRAP? BILL TURNER?

8

"WHY ALL THIS TROUBLE FOR SPARROW'S FREEDOM?"

15

16

SHE IS THE ONLY PERSON JACK CAN ASK FOR HELP!

I BROUGHT PAYMENT!

SCREECH, SCREECH!

WE'RE LOOKING FOR THIS KEY— AND WHAT IT GOES TO!

THAT COMPASS YOU BARTERED FROM ME CAN'T LEAD YOU TO THIS, JACK?

JACK SPARROW DOES NOT KNOW WHAT HE WANTS?

HMPF!

YOUR KEY GOES TO A CHEST . . . AND IT IS WHAT'S INSIDE THIS CHEST YOU SEEK.

YOU KNOW OF DAVY JONES? A GREAT SAILOR . . . UNTIL HE FELL IN LOVE.

I HEARD IT WAS THE SEA.

IT WAS A WOMAN, AS UNTAMABLE AS THE SEA. HE NEVER STOPPED LOVING HER, AND THE PAIN WAS TOO MUCH TO LIVE WITH . . .

. . . BUT NOT ENOUGH TO CAUSE HIM TO DIE!

WHAT IS IN THE CHEST?

HIS HEART!

HE CARVED IT OUT, LOCKED IT AWAY, AND HID IT FROM THE WORLD. THE KEY IS WITH HIM AT ALL TIMES!

SLIP ABOARD THE *FLYING DUTCHMAN*, TAKE THE KEY, AND THEN YOU CAN GO BACK AND SAVE YOUR BONNY LASS, WILL.

LET ME SEE YOUR HAND!

THE BLACK SPOT!

SCREEK

THIS WILL HELP YOU.

SCREECH! SCREECH!

DAVY JONES CANNOT STEP ON LAND BUT ONCE EVERY TEN YEARS . . .

LAND IS WHERE YOU ARE SAFE, SO CARRY LAND WITH YOU!

A JAR OF DIRT?

IT WILL HELP.

WE NEED TO FIND THE *FLYING DUTCHMAN.*

TLACK TLACK TLACK

THANKS TO TIA DALMA, THEY KNOW WHERE TO GO . . .

. . . AND WHAT TO LOOK FOR!

22

24

25

SHHH! IS THERE SOMETHING THAT CAN SAVE WILL?

YES. THERE IS A CHEST THAT CONTAINS THE STILL-BEATING HEART OF DAVY JONES. WHOEVER HAS THE CHEST, HAS THE LEVERAGE TO SAVE OUR WILLIAM FROM HIS FATE!

HOW CAN WE FIND IT?

THIS COMPASS POINTS TO WHAT YOU WANT MOST IN THIS WORLD . . .

. . . AND WHAT *YOU* WANT MOST IN THIS WORLD IS TO FIND THE CHEST OF DAVY JONES.

TO SAVE WILL!

THE *BLACK PEARL* FINALLY HAS ITS HEADING.

AND ON THE *FLYING DUTCHMAN* . . .

THAT'S FIVE FROM THE LASH!

I'LL TAKE IT ALL.

AND WHAT WOULD PROMPT SUCH ACT OF CHARITY, BOOTSTRAP?

MY SON . . . *THAT'S MY SON!*

ON THE *FLYING DUTCHMAN*, SAILORS PLAY DICE, BETTING YEARS OF SERVICE.

WILL CHALLENGES DAVY JONES TO A GAME!

SLAM

I WAGER MY SOUL! I BID EIGHT SIXES!

AGAINST?

I WANT YOUR KEY!

HOW DO YOU KNOW OF THE KEY?

I'M JOINING THE GAME! I WAGER A LIFETIME OF SERVICE, AND I BID TWELVE SIXES!

SLAM

CLEVER. MY ONLY CHOICE IS TO DEFEAT YOU, AND NOT YOUR SON.

BOOTSTRAP BILL, YOU OWE A LIFETIME OF SERVICE!

WHY DID YOU DO THAT?

I COULDN'T LET YOU LOSE.

28

29

33

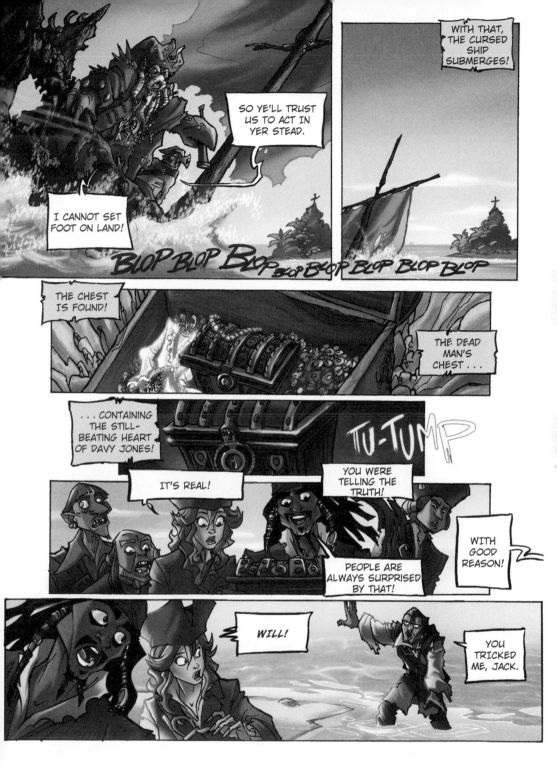

35

HAVE YOU ALL FALLEN IN LEAGUE WITH THIS SCOUNDREL?

WE THOUGHT SPARROW WAS TRYING TO SAVE YOUR LIFE.

WELL, I OWE YOU THANKS, JACK. I WAS REUNITED WITH MY FATHER ON JONES'S SHIP.

I PROMISED HIM I'D KILL JONES.

THEN WHO WILL CALL HIS BEASTIE OFF THE HUNT?

SWISS

I KEEP MY PROMISES, JACK.

CLANG

SWISS

LORD BECKETT DESIRES THAT CHEST. I INTEND TO DELIVER IT TO HIM!

ELIZABETH, GUARD THE CHEST!

HOW'D THIS HAPPEN?

EACH WANTS THE CHEST FOR HIMSELF. WILL ON ACCOUNT OF HIS FATHER; NORRINGTON TO REGAIN HIS HONOR; JACK PLANS ON TRADIN' IT TO JONES TO CALL OFF THE KRAKEN!

HAH-HAH!

WHILE WILL AND NORRINGTON RUN AFTER JACK AND THE KEY, DAVY JONES'S MEN ARRIVE.

NORRINGTON TAKES THE CHEST, DRAWING JONES'S UNBEATABLE HOARD AWAY FROM JACK, ELIZABETH, AND WILL. A NOBLE SACRIFICE . . . ?

HERE YOU GO.

HEH, HEH!

PERHAPS NOT SO NOBLE AFTER ALL.

MINUTES LATER, ON THE *BLACK PEARL* . . .

NO DANGER. I SEE EMPTY HORIZON IN ALL DIRECTIONS!

41

42

44

46